RABBITS

Joanne Randolph

PowerKiDS press™

New York

Published in 2007 by The Rosen Publishing Group, Inc.
29 East 21st Street, New York, NY 10010

First Edition

Book Design: Julio Gil

Photo Credits: All images Shutterstock.com.

Library of Congress Cataloging-in-Publication Data

Randolph, Joanne.
  Rabbits / Joanne Randolph. — 1st ed.
      p. cm. — (Classroom pets)
  Includes bibliographical references and index.
  ISBN-13: 978-1-4042-3680-6 (library binding)
  ISBN-10: 1-4042-3680-5 (library binding)
  1. Rabbits—Juvenile literature. 2. Rabbits—Study and teaching (Elementary)—Activity programs—Juvenile literature. I. Title.
  SF453.2.R36 2007
  636.9'322—dc22

                                        2006030509

Manufactured in the United States of America

Contents

Picking a Rabbit for Your Classroom

Your class has decided to welcome a rabbit into your room. Having a pet in the classroom can be a treat. Have you decided what kind of rabbit you want? There are more than 100 **breeds** of rabbit from which to pick. The breeds are grouped based on size, hair type and length, whether their ears stand up straight or flop down, and color.

Be sure to pick a young rabbit that is over seven weeks old. Try to pick a rabbit that likes people and the other rabbits in its cage. You will want to be sure your new pet is healthy, too.

A healthy rabbit has bright, clear eyes and shiny fur. The rabbit should also have clean ears and a dry nose.

5

About Rabbits

Rabbits make friendly, happy pets. However, most rabbits are not raised for this purpose. Rabbits are commonly raised as food, for their fur, or to be used for **medical research**. It is a very lucky rabbit that gets to become part of a family or classroom as a pet! Your class is lucky, too. Rabbits are easy to care for and can be very loving.

Wild rabbits were kept in pens as food animals as early as 3,000 years ago. They were first **domesticated** around 2,000 years ago. You and your classmates can learn a lot from your new pet.

This girl is holding her pet rabbit. Most rabbits are friendly and like to be held and to spend time with their owners.

One Rabbit or Two?

Wild rabbits are friendly animals. They live in groups called **colonies**. Pet rabbits are happiest when they live with another rabbit or a small group of rabbits, too. If you decide to get one rabbit, you need to give the rabbit lots of attention.

If you decide to get more than one rabbit, there are a few things to keep in mind. Rabbits can make lots of babies quickly. If you keep a pair of rabbits, two females might be best. Male rabbits can be kept together, too, but they must be **neutered** to keep them from fighting.

A rabbit under three months old will likely have no trouble getting used to a new friend. Older rabbits need more time.

A Place to Call Home

Before your rabbit comes to class for the first time, you will need to get its home ready. Rabbits will be happy in almost any home you make. Be sure your pet has enough space, though. The bottom of the cage should be deep enough to keep the bedding inside when the rabbit digs or moves. The top of the cage should be **metal**.

Spread soft pieces of wood, called wood chips, on the bottom of the cage. Then cover the chips with straw. Your pet's new home is ready!

Your rabbit should also be given a box in which to hide and sleep.
This will help your new pet feel safe.

Let's Eat

Your new pet should be fed twice a day. In the morning feed the rabbit dry food. This food can be placed in a bowl on the cage floor. In the afternoon the rabbit should be fed greens and other fresh foods. Fresh hay should always be available in a rack fixed to the wall of the cage. Water should also always be available.

What are some of the foods a rabbit likes best? You will have a happy pet if you give it parsley, dandelion greens, field greens, carrots with greens, and apples and other fruits.

These rabbits are checking out their food dish
to see what is for dinner.

Holding Your Pet

Most rabbits like to be held and petted. Give your rabbit a chance to get used to its new home first, though. You and your classmates should start by getting to know your rabbit through the cage walls.

Once the rabbit has settled in and your teacher says it is OK, you can softly pick up and hold the rabbit. Always let the rabbit smell your hands first. Never pick the rabbit up suddenly from above. This is how birds catch and eat rabbits.

Rabbits need to be let out of the cage to play each day.

Rabbit Talk

You might think that your new pet does not say much. Rabbits let us know what they are thinking in many ways, though. Rabbits use their bodies to talk to each other and to us. They also use **scents** and sounds.

If a rabbit sits up on its back legs, it is wondering what is happening nearby. If your rabbit presses its body to the floor, it is scared. A rabbit sitting quietly with its ears back is resting. If the rabbit **growls**, watch out! It may bite.

A rabbit may grunt if you do something it does not like. You may hear this sound if you try to put your pet back in its cage before it is ready.

Fun and Games

A happy rabbit needs to run, play, and jump. You can make fun **obstacle courses** to give your rabbit the exercise it needs. Place things like blocks, stones, cans, or wood along the wall. You can use treats to show your rabbit what it should do.

You can also place lots of boxes with holes in them around the room. The rabbit will have fun looking and climbing inside. You may also give your rabbit a box filled with ripped paper. The rabbit can dig and roll around in the box. Be **creative**. Your rabbit will thank you!

All rabbits like to play. This dwarf rabbit looks forward to some playtime as its owner takes it from its cage.

Your new pet is counting on you to take care of it. Everyone in the class needs to do his or her part to keep the rabbit happy and healthy. Some things that can cause illness are changing its food or giving it food that is not fresh. Not giving the rabbit enough water is also a cause of sickness. Wetness or air that is too hot can make your rabbit sick, too. You must also make sure the cage is kept clean and dry.

If you see that your rabbit is acting unwell, let your teacher know. He or she may need to bring your pet to the **veterinarian**.

This is a healthy young rabbit. Its fur looks clean and flat,
and its eyes are bright and clear.

It can be great fun to own a rabbit. It is also a full-time job. You and your classmates need to decide who will feed the rabbit, brush its fur, and clean the litter box. You must also talk about who will take the rabbit home on the weekends and for vacations.

Sharing your class with a rabbit is also a great chance to learn. Think of questions you have about rabbits. Look up the answers. Share what you find out with your classmates. Keep a log of what your rabbit does each day. Have fun getting to know your new pet.

Glossary

breeds (BREEDZ) Groups of animals that look alike and have the same kin.

colonies (KAH-luh-neez) Groups that live together.

creative (kree-AY-tiv) Having different, new ideas.

domesticated (duh-MES-tih-kayt-id) Raised to live with people.

growls (GRAW-ulz) Makes a low sound often made as a sign by an animal that it may bite if not left alone.

medical (MEH-duh-kul) Having to do with fighting illness.

metal (MEH-tul) Hard matter that is shiny, hard, and can easily be shaped.

neutered (NOO-terd) Fixed so that an animal cannot make babies.

obstacle courses (OB-stih-kul KORS-ez) Paths that are lined with things that must be jumped or climbed.

research (REE-serch) Careful study.

scents (SENTS) Things that are sensed by the nose.

veterinarian (veh-tuh-ruh-NER-ee-un) A doctor who treats animals.

Index

Web Sites

Due to the changing nature of Internet links, PowerKids Press has developed an online list of Web sites related to this book. This site is updated regularly. Please use this link to access the list:
www.powerkidslinks.com/cpets/rabbit/